Richard Scarry's
Great Big
SCHOOLHOUSE

ABRIDGED EDITION

Written and illustrated by Richard Scarry

 RANDOM HOUSE NEW YORK

Abridged Edition. Copyright © 1969, 1979 by Richard Scarry. All rights reserved under International and Pan-American Copyright Conventions. Published in the United States by Random House, Inc., New York, and simultaneously in Canada by Random House of Canada Limited, Toronto. This title was originally cataloged by the Library of Congress as follows: Scarry, Richard. Richard Scarry's great big schoolhouse, written and illustrated by Richard Scarry. New York, Random House, [1969] 69 p. col. illus. 33 cm. 2.95 An account of all that Huckle Cat did and learned during a school day. [1. Animals—Stories. 2. School stories] I. Title PZ10.3.S287Ri [Fic] 74–90292 ISBN: 0–394–80874–6 (trade); 0–394–90874–0 (lib. bdg.). Manufactured in the United States of America. 2 3 4 5 6 7 8 9 0

Getting Ready for School

Huckle's mother woke him up.
"It is time to get up for school," she said.
"Why do I have to go to school?" asked Huckle.
"All children go to school to learn how to read and write," said his mother. "You want to be able to read and write, don't you? Now please get up."

blanket

Huckle got up. He yawned and rubbed the sleep out of his eyes. He walked to the bathroom.

mirror

sink

towel

soap

He washed his face
with soap and warm water.

pajamas

toothpaste

He brushed his teeth.

comb

He combed his hair
with cold water.

cap

suspenders

shirt

underpants

suit jacket

overcoat

play jacket

overalls

rain hat

raincoat

sneakers

shoes

gloves

mittens

rubber boots

socks

Then Huckle got dressed.
That is NOT the way to put on your pants, Huckle!

bowl · brief case · teapot · tablecloth · cup · saucer · fork · knife · spoon

Mother Cat served hot cereal to Huckle for his breakfast.
Lowly Worm stopped by on his way to school.
"Hurry or you will be late for school," he said.

bacon · eggs · glass

"LATE! My goodness! I am late for work," said Father Cat.
He picked up his briefcase and ran.
Oh dear! He picked up the tablecloth, too!

Mother Cat walked with Huckle to the school bus stop.
Honk! Honk! The school bus came to take the children
to school.

Riding on the School Bus

black train locomotive

red and green coach

Every day Huckle rides to school in his orange school bus. He sees many colorful things.
Everything has a color.
What color is the fisherman's suit?

purple jeep

STOP

manhole

SCHOOL BUS

street

red motorcycle

Gorilla Bananas and his yellow Banana-mobile

BUGDOZER

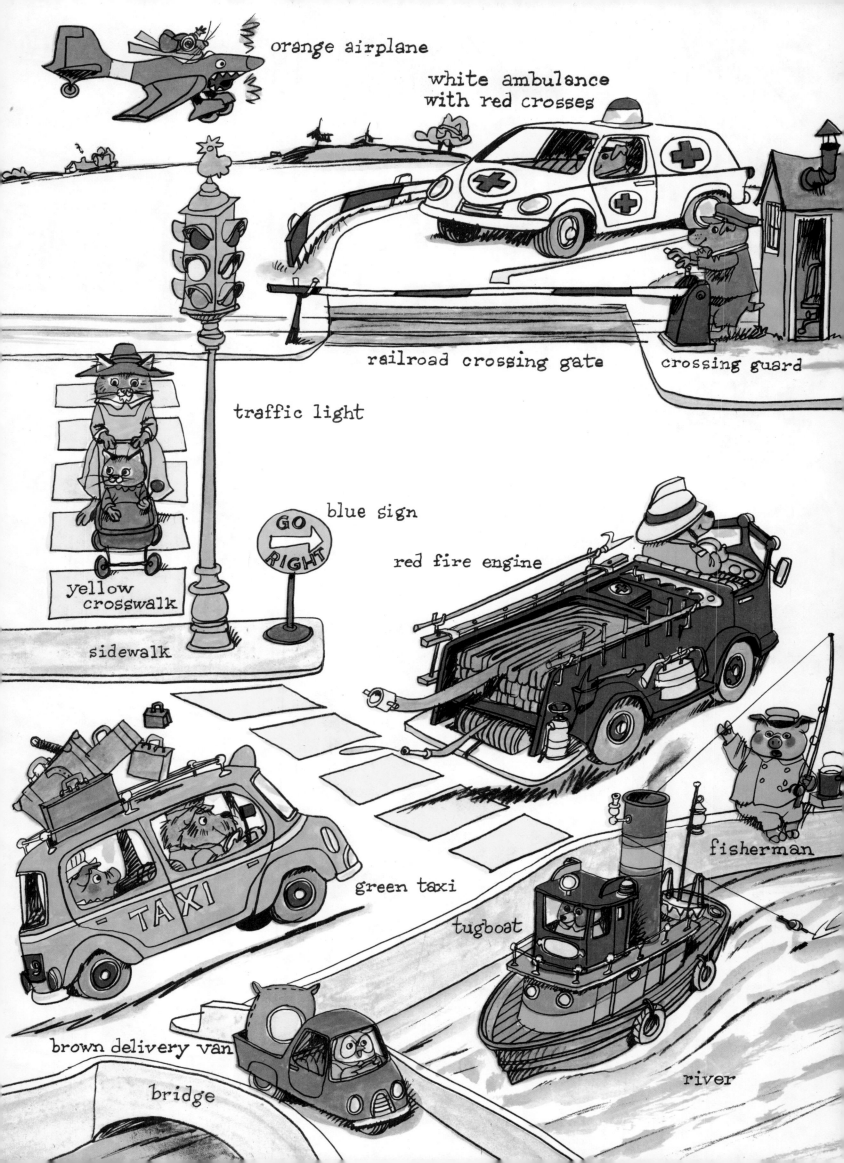

orange airplane

white ambulance
with red crosses

railroad crossing gate

crossing guard

traffic light

blue sign

red fire engine

yellow
crosswalk

sidewalk

green taxi

fisherman

tugboat

brown delivery van

bridge

river

GO
RIGHT

TAXI

weather vane

postman

bell

The School

This is Huckle's school.
The school bus stopped in the schoolyard.
The school bell rang.
It was time for school to begin.
But what was all that noise outside?

clock
tower

CENTRAL
SCHOOL

principal's office

schoolyard

policeman

chimney sweep

school crossing guard

School library

classroom

classroom

classroom

classroom

classroom

doctor's office

Why, it was Joe, the janitor!
As usual he was late for school.

SCHOOL BUS

SCHOOL BUS

balloon

alphabet

Aa *Aa* | Bb *Bb* | Cc *Cc* | Dd *Da*

string

clock

bell

wall

notice board

calendar

SEPTEMBER

SUN	MON	TUES	WED	THU	FRI	SAT
		1	2	3	4	5
6	7	8	9	10	11	12
13	14	15	16	17	18	19
20	21	22	23	24	25	26
27	28	29	30			

teacher

map

umbrella

overshoes

desk

pupils

The Classroom

This is Huckle's classroom.
And behind the big desk sits Miss Honey, his teacher.
Every morning the pupils say, "Good morning, Miss Honey."
And every morning she says, "Good morning, children.
My, don't you look bright and fresh this morning!"
She always says that.

LEARNING THE ALPHABET

Aa Bb Cc Dd Ee Ff Gg Hh Ii Jj Kk Ll
Mm Nn Oo Pp Qq Rr Ss Tt Uu Vv Ww Xx Yy Zz

Each day Miss Honey teaches her class something new.
Today she was going to teach them the alphabet.
She gave each child a card with one of the letters
of the alphabet on it. Everyone tried to think of words
that began with the letters on the cards.

yum yum!

A is the first letter of the alphabet.
Arthur Pig brought an apple for the teacher.
He also brought one for our friend, Lowly Worm.

apple

broom

bowl

book

bench

"Bananas Gorilla! Take that Bananamobile back
outside where it belongs!" said Miss Honey.
"And please eat your breakfast at home!"

boot

banana

Charles Anteater drew a car with his crayon.
He showed it to the class.

Donald Walrus danced up and down on his desk.
Did you see the drawer pop out?

Elizabeth emptied her purse
and found some earrings.
She put them on.
They were extra heavy.

fountain

faucet

furniture

Frances Raccoon showed the children her doll furniture.
Lowly Worm turned on the bathtub faucet and pretended
to be a fountain.

green string

glass beads

Gloria Fox strung glass beads on a green string.
She forgot that there are two ends to a piece of string.
Bugdozer gathered up the runaway beads.

Honk!

hat

head

horn

Keep your nose up!

Huckle blew hard on his horn.
Lowly was hiding inside it. Now Lowly knows how to fly!

I can fly as straight
as an arrow!

Indian

Irving Goat is pretending
he is an Indian.

J j

Jimmy Crocodile spread orange juice on his bread
and poured jam in his glass.
Now just a minute! Isn't that wrong?

K k

kerchief

How do you get it to come out?

ketchup

bread knife   sharp kitchen knives   tea kettle

Kathy is wearing a kerchief. Lowly is shaking the ketchup.
Kathy is showing us things that are used in the kitchen.
Never touch sharp kitchen knives.

L l

All right, Lowly!
How many things can you name
that begin with the letter "L"?

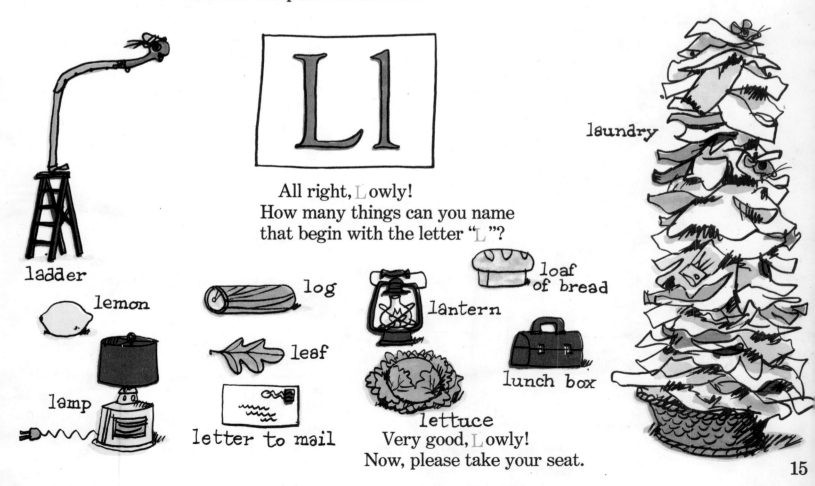

ladder

lemon

log

lantern

loaf of bread

laundry

leaf

lamp

letter to mail

lettuce

lunch box

Very good, Lowly!
Now, please take your seat.

melon

Mm

Mildred Hippo is a magician.
She can make things disappear.
She put a melon in her mouth.
She munched on it.
It disappeared! Mmmm! Good!
My! What a marvelous trick!

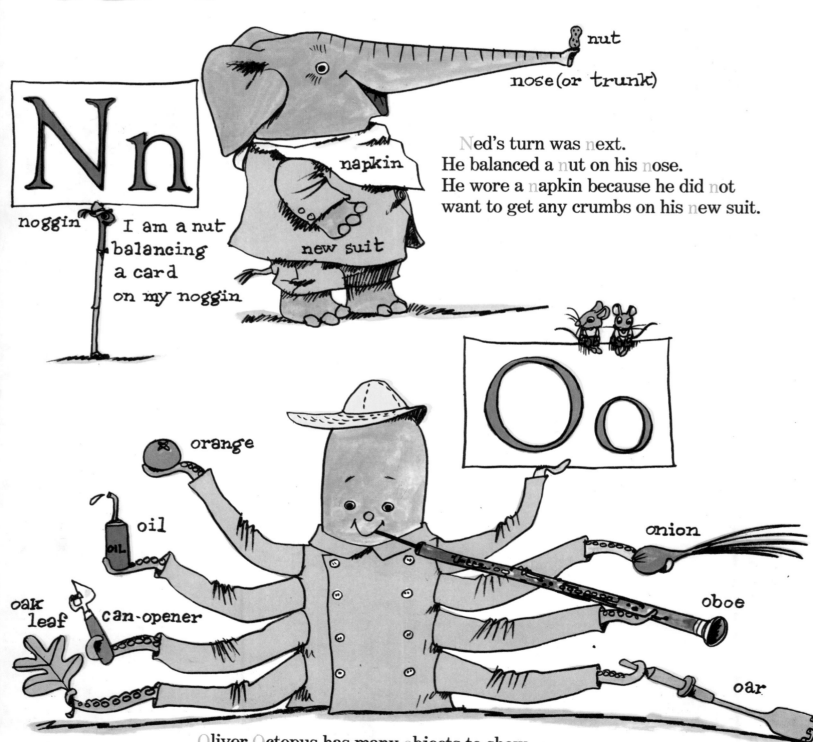

nut

nose (or trunk)

Nn

napkin

Ned's turn was next.
He balanced a nut on his nose.
He wore a napkin because he did not
want to get any crumbs on his new suit.

noggin

I am a nut
balancing
a card
on my noggin

new suit

Oo

orange

oil

onion

oak
leaf

can-opener

oboe

oar

Oliver Octopus has many objects to show.
He often forgets to take off his overcoat in the classroom.
He played an old lullaby on his oboe.

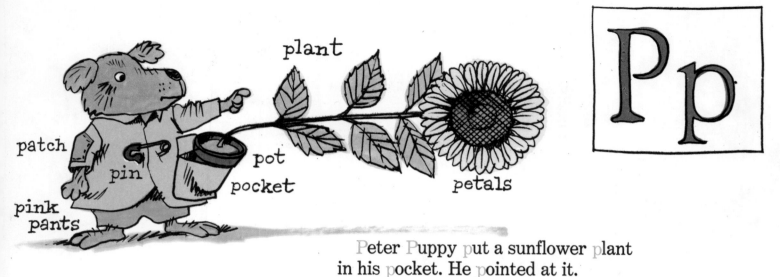

plant

patch

pin

pocket

pot

pink pants

petals

P p

Peter Puppy put a sunflower plant in his pocket. He pointed at it.

Q q

whole pie

1 2 3

quarter piece

4

Please be quiet, children. Oswald Owl has a question to ask you.
"How many quarter pieces of pie are there in one whole pie?"
You are quite right! Each whole pie can be divided into four quarters.

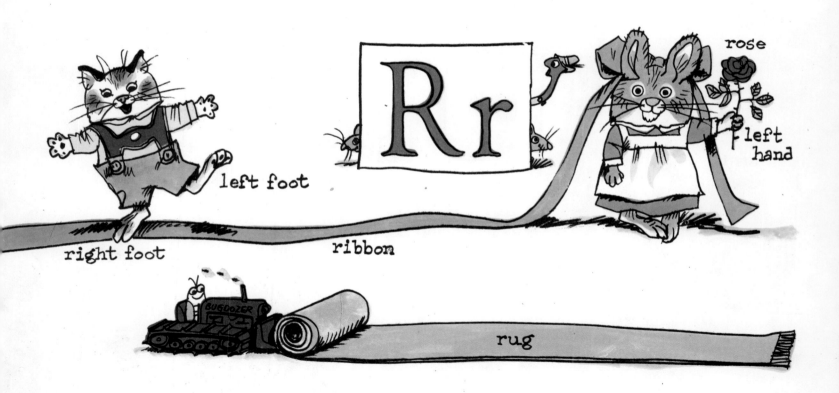

R r

rose

left hand

left foot

right foot

ribbon

rug

Ruth Rabbit has a ribbon in her hair.
She has a rose in her left hand.
Huckle has a ribbon under his right foot.
Bugdozer is rolling up the rug.

Spotty Leopard showed his schoolmates a tube of paste.
He squeezed it. It squirted. It made a spot. Paste is sticky.
Miss Honey told Spotty to get some soap and water.

Tom Tiger told everyone how to tie a knot.
He took two pieces of twine and tied them together.

Ursula Pig stays
under her umbrella
when it rains.
She has used it a lot.

Victor Bear showed some pretty violets
and a vine in a vase. He tripped on the vine.

Willy Fox can't think of one word that begins with a "W". Can you help him?

What am I? I am a worm wagon! Watch me wiggle!

wheel

watch

Lowly showed the class how he plays the xylophone with one foot.

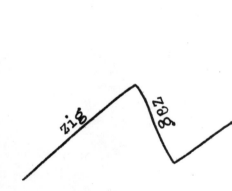

Yvonne dropped an egg on the floor so everyone could see the yellow yolk inside.

zig zag

Lowly walked zigzag.

"Very good!" said Miss Honey. "Now, let us all recite our ABC's! Begin!"

"ABCD... EFG... HIJK... LMN... O. P. QRS... TUV... W... X..Y..Z

Now I've said my ABC's; tell me what you think of me"

Making Things

Miss Honey showed us how to make all kinds of exciting things with a few simple materials and tools.

embroidery

needle

yarn

weaving

Kathy embroidered
with a needle and yarn.

Penny is a weaver.
She wove a table mat.

paste

magazine

scrapbook

crayon

coloring book

Huckle cut pictures out of old
magazines and made a scrapbook.

Charlie colored a coloring
book with crayons.

knitting nancy

a sweater!

stringing beads

Frances knit a sweater for Lowly.

Ruth strung beads on a string.

modeling clay

Willy modeled a bunny
with modeling clay.

building blocks

Robert built a tower with building blocks.
Stop, Robert! That is enough!

making things with paper

paper airplanes

Mary cut out pieces of paper
and folded them.
She made a doll house.

Arthur folded paper, too. He made
paper airplanes. ARTHUR PIG! You know
better than to throw things in class!

Recess on the Playground

Every day the children have recess. Recess is a time for play.
When the weather is nice they play in the schoolyard.

rings

swing

sliding pole

hurt knee

climbing ladder

shovel

pail

barrel

hide and seek

sand box

ring-a-round-a-rosie

kicking a ball

marbles

jacks

see saw

slide

ring toss

leap frog

tag

catching a ball

jump rope

pat·a·cake

hop scotch

stilts

23

The Days of the Week

SUNDAY MONDAY TUESDAY WEDNESDAY THURSDAY FRIDAY SATURDAY

At school, Miss Honey teaches us many things.
When she is not teaching, she is very busy doing other things.

On **Sunday** afternoon she drove out into the
country with her friend Mr. Bruno to have a picnic.
Picnics are always fun. Don't you think so?

On **Monday** after school she did her laundry.

On **Tuesday** morning before school, she baked
a cake for the sick children in the hospital.

Mother Cat took it to them.

On **Wednesday** she made up packages of used clothing to send to children who do not have enough to wear.

On **Thursday** she met with the principal and the other teachers to plan a school picnic.

On **Friday** she went to the library to read books and study. She is always learning new things to teach her children.

On **Saturday** she did her marketing. And on Saturday night she invited Mr. Bruno for supper. He always brings flowers when he visits. After supper he took Miss Honey to the movies.

You are a very busy lady, Miss Honey!

LEARNING TO COUNT

0 1 2 3 4 5
zero none one two three four five

6 7 8 9 10
six seven eight nine ten

0
Zero none

stool

"Now we shall learn how to count," said Miss Honey.
"Huckle will hold the card showing the correct answer.
How many children are sitting on the stool?" she asked.
The answer is **none.** There is no one sitting there.
We use the figure **zero** to show **none.**

flower

1
one

vase

How many flowers are
in the vase on Miss Honey's desk?
You are right, Huckle.
There is just **one** flower.

2
two

When those little girls stop
talking, how many quiet girls
will there be?
There will be **two** quiet girls
when they stop talking.

Roger Raccoon drew a picture of the teacher,
a picture of Huckle, and a picture of Lowly.
If you say he drew **three** pictures, you are right!

Arthur Pig had some big marbles in his pocket.
His pocket ripped open and they fell out.
One, two, three, **four. Four** bouncing marbles.

Miss Honey asked Willy Fox to take the wastebaskets out
and empty them. But, Willy, don't take them all at once!
Empty the **five** wastebaskets one at a time! One, two, three, four, **five.**

Well! What a mess Willy made!
How many brooms did the class use to clean it up?
Six brooms is the right answer.

one　　two　　three　　four　　five　　six

Now, why are all those children raising their hands?
It's because they want to ask Miss Honey for permission
to go to the bathroom. You always have to ask, you know.
"All right, you may go. But hurry back," said the teacher.
Seven children left the room to go to the bathroom.

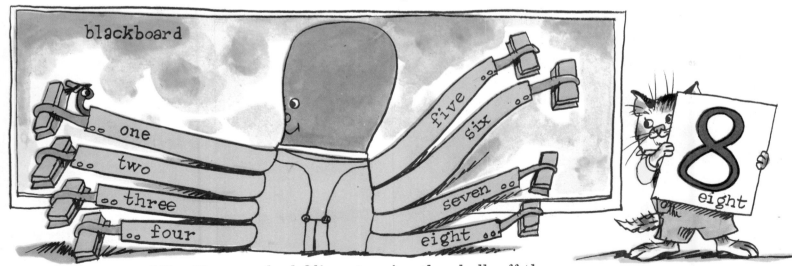

Miss Honey asked Oliver to wipe the chalk off the
blackboard with the erasers. How many erasers did he use?
He has **eight** arms so he used **eight** erasers.

By the time the blackboard was wiped clean,
the erasers were full of chalk dust.
Miss Honey asked some children to clap the erasers
to clean them. How many are clapping erasers?

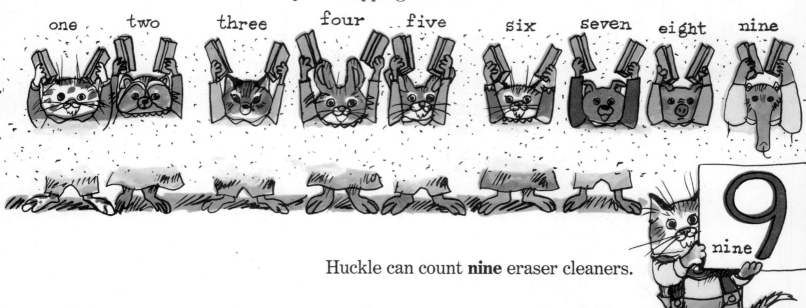

one   two   three   four   five   six   seven   eight   nine

Huckle can count **nine** eraser cleaners.

Miss Honey asked Bananas Gorilla what
he brought to school to eat at snack time.
Did he bring **ten** bananas?
NO! He brought **ten** bunches of bananas!

one   two   three   four   five

six   seven   eight   nine   ten

My! He does like bananas! Now let us all count from **one** to **ten**.
One, two, three, four, five, six, seven, eight, nine, ten.
Very good, children!

The Hours of the Day

It was Saturday. There was no school.
But there were lots of things for Huckle to do.
His friend Lowly was coming to visit for the day.
He was going to stay overnight, too.

At **7** o'clock Huckle bounced out of bed.

At **8** o'clock he ate his breakfast.
Father Cat took the tablecloth to work with him again.

At **9** o'clock he straightened out his room.

At **10** o'clock he
went shopping for food.

At **11** o'clock he played in
his muddy yard with Lowly.
He fell down a few times.

12 o'clock is noontime.
Huckle and Lowly ate their lunches.
Lowly remembered to take his hat off
at the table.

At **1** o'clock they both lay down
and had a nap.

At **2** o'clock they went for a ride.
They bumped into Joe, the school janitor.
He was on his way to school and he was late again.

At **3** o'clock they walked home.

At **4** o'clock they watched television.

At **5** o'clock
Father Cat came home.

At **6** o'clock Mother Cat served a surprise for supper. She served Huckle's guest first.

At **7** o'clock Father Cat gave Huckle and Lowly their baths. "Where did that soap go?" asked Father Cat.

At **8** o'clock Father Cat read them a bedtime story in bed.

And at **9** o'clock they were sound asleep.
Sleep tight, Huckle!
Sleep tight, Lowly!

Miss Honey's Busy Helpers

Everyone helps in little ways to make Miss Honey's life happier.
Miss Honey will never forget the day when Lowly polished her apple.

That same day Roger opened
the window and the papers blew away.

Arthur closed the door so
they wouldn't escape.

Miss Honey remembers that
Huckle sharpened the pencils that day.
He made them a little too short.

Patsy picked papers up off the floor
and put them in the wastebasket.

Eddie erased
the blackboard.

Peter washed the
blackboard with a sponge.

Bobby clapped the erasers.
Miss Honey was about to tell him
to clean them outside when . . .

. . . she saw that someone was watering her plant!

"STOP IT!" she cried.

Why, it was another of her busy helpers!
Joe, the janitor! He had been washing
the outside of her windows.
  "Did I get you a little wet?" he asked. "You forgot
to tell someone to close the window!"
  OH, JOE! You should have looked!

37

Measuring Things

"Now we shall learn something about how to measure things," said Miss Honey.

I use a ruler to measure my height.
I am **taller** than Bugdozer.
He is **shorter** than I am.

ruler

I use a scale to measure my weight.
I weigh **more** than Lowly.
He weighs **less** than I do.
I am **heavier** than he is.
He is **lighter** than I am.

scales

My arm is **longer** than Mouse's.
His arm is **shorter** than mine.

A clock measures time.
I awakened **before** the sun came up.

Huckle awakened **after** the sun came up.
I have been awake a **longer** time than Huckle.
He has been awake a **shorter** time than I have.

hot
warm
cool
cold

For breakfast I had a **hot** cup of cocoa.
Huckle had a **cold** glass of milk.

hot
warm
cool
cold

stove

refrigerator

We make things **warm** on the stove.

We keep things **cool** in the refrigerator.

A calendar measures time, too.
It shows the number of days
in the month and the year.

I have had more birthdays than Ruth.
I am **older** than she is.
Ruth is **younger** than I am.

My birthday cake has
more candles than Ruth's.
Hers has **fewer** candles than mine.
I have a **harder** time
blowing out the candles
than Ruth does.
Ruth has an **easier** time.

Shapes

"Everything has a shape," said Miss Honey.
"I will show you different kinds of shapes.
First, look at my shape. Mr. Bruno says
I have a beautiful shape. Would you say
that I was **fatter** or **thinner** than Lowly?
Yes! I am a little bit **fatter** than Lowly."

Lowly has been eating peas.
Peas are round in shape.

A ball is round, too.
But Lowly isn't able to eat that.

A block has a square shape.

An egg is oval-shaped.

The moon is sometimes crescent-shaped.

Oh, yes! Someone sent me a
Valentine in the shape of a heart.
Can you guess who sent it?

To
Miss Honey
from
Bruno

diamond

bell

triangle

star

circle

cone

I have asked Huckle to draw some more shapes for you to see.

straight

curved

crooked

And also some lines. Thank you, Huckle.

Now, some things change their shape.
A large candle becomes small.

A short seedling becomes
a tall sunflower.

great

large   small

tiny

it's magic!

smoke

fire

And a burning piece of wood turns
to smoke and ashes.
Can you think of anything else that
changes its shape?
A snowman, maybe? When?

wood

Drawing and Painting

Drawing and painting are always fun.
On drawing and painting days Miss Honey's class is full of artists.
Some artists draw pictures with crayons or pencils.
Some paint pictures with paint and water.
All of them wear smocks so that they won't
get their clothes messy.

Huckle helped the teacher pass out
the drawing and painting materials.

These are some of the things he handed to the artists.

pencils

eraser

ball-point pen

pencil sharpener

marker pen

sheets of paper

crayons

paint jars

water dish

mixing tray

pastels

paint brush

paint box

At last everyone was ready.

Mildred Hippo placed a pad of paper on her easel. She drew a bug with her pencil.

easel

My Doll

Elizabeth Rabbit drew a picture with her pastels. She tacked it on the wall.

Arthur Pig painted a red apple on the paper.

picture

paint water

Bobby Cat painted some red footprints on the floor.

Roger Raccoon went to the sink to wash the dirty paint water out of his water dish. He ran the water too hard. He made a spatter painting.

sink

My! What a busy group of artists!

43

Color

Huckle will show some of the things he has painted.

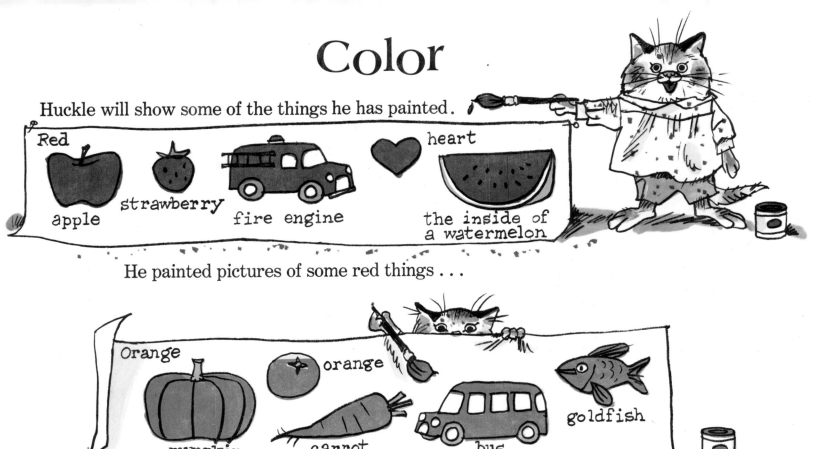

Red
apple
strawberry
fire engine
heart
the inside of a watermelon

He painted pictures of some red things . . .

Orange
pumpkin
orange
carrot
bus
goldfish

. . . and some orange things.

Yellow
daffodil
banana
corn
lemon
cheese
bell

Yellow is a bright sunny color.

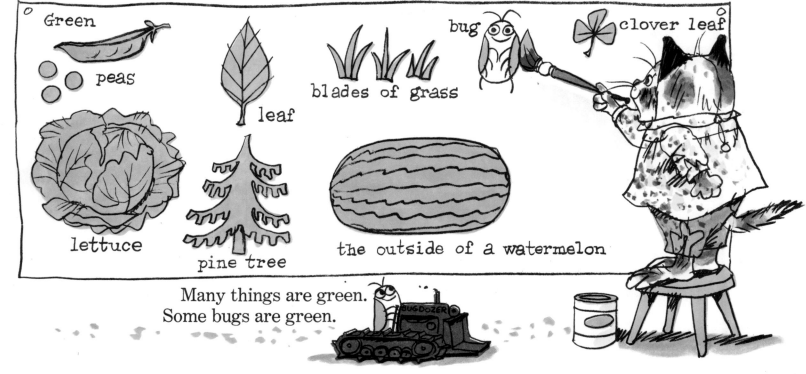

Green
peas
leaf
blades of grass
bug
clover leaf
lettuce
pine tree
the outside of a watermelon

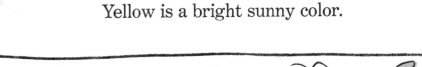

Many things are green.
Some bugs are green.

Blue

cloud sky

blueberries

bluebells

sailboat

Huckle painted a blue sky.
When it is cloudy, the sky is colored gray.
Be careful, Huckle!

Violet – Purple

violet

plum

thistle

pansy

grapes

Huckle painted the floor violet.
Purple is almost the same color as violet.

Brown

walnut

potato

shoelace

chocolate
Easter Bunny

light   dark

Colors can be light or dark. A potato is light brown.
A chocolate Easter bunny is dark brown.

Black   doorbell

gumdrop

hat

tire

White

egg

snowman

He painted some black things . . .   . . . and some white ones.

Besides painting pictures, Huckle painted himself.
Wash the paint off, Huckle, and put on a clean smock. Thank you!

Mixing Colors

Huckle will now show how to mix two colors together to make a third color! Begin, Huckle!

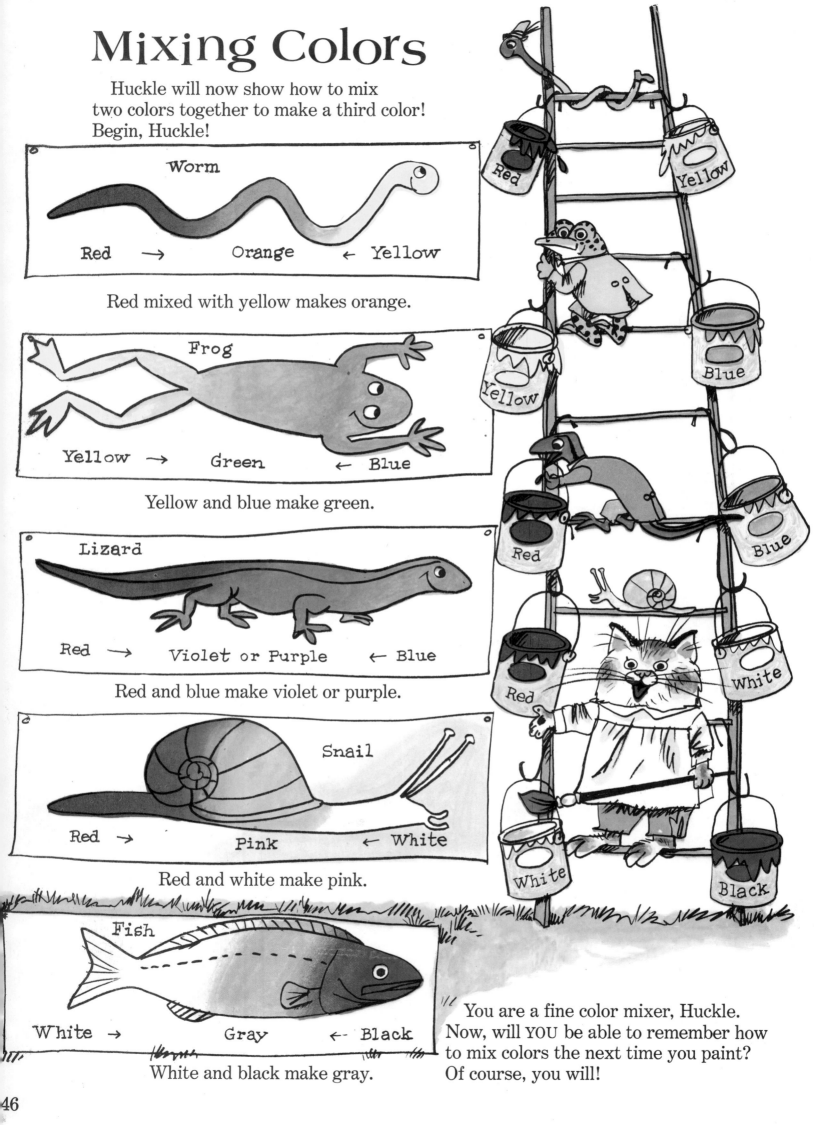

Worm

Red → Orange ← Yellow

Red mixed with yellow makes orange.

Frog

Yellow → Green ← Blue

Yellow and blue make green.

Lizard

Red → Violet or Purple ← Blue

Red and blue make violet or purple.

Snail

Red → Pink ← White

Red and white make pink.

Fish

White → Gray ← Black

White and black make gray.

You are a fine color mixer, Huckle. Now, will YOU be able to remember how to mix colors the next time you paint? Of course, you will!

46

Show and Tell

One of the best times at school
is "Show and Tell" time.
Huckle is going to tell about the
exciting time he had last summer
when he visited his Uncle Willie's farm.
Let's listen.

Huckle started to tell his story.
"Well, first of all," he said, "I had to get
to my uncle's farm. My mother and father took me
to the airport and put me on an airplane.

"I flew to another airport near my uncle's farm.
My uncle was waiting for me on the airport runway.
We almost landed on top of him!

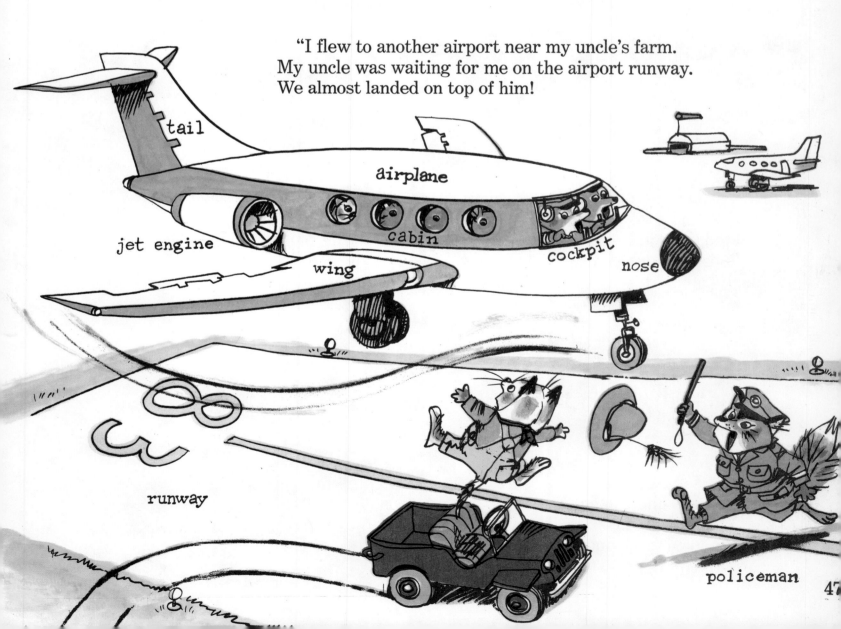

tail

airplane

jet engine

cabin

cockpit

nose

wing

runway

policeman

"We drove to Uncle Willie's farm," said Huckle.
"When we got there, my Aunt Millie was cooking
in the kitchen. She is a good cook.

cock·a·doodle·doo   rooster

chicken house

hen

"Hens and roosters are chickens.
Hens have to eat before they will lay eggs.
I fed them grain and corn. Uncle Willie gathered the eggs.
Roosters don't lay eggs. They crow. Cock-a-doodle-doo!

cow barn

"I fed hay to the cows.
Cows make milk.
Uncle Willie milked them.
We put the cans of milk in
the farm truck and drove to the dairy.

farmhouse

MILK   MILK   MILK

"At the dairy many things are done with the milk.
Some milk is put in cartons and sold at the market for drinking.
Some milk is made into butter. Some is made into cheese.
And, best of all, some is made into ice cream. The dairy man gave me an ice cream cone.

"Then we went back to the farm
and plowed a field to make it
ready for planting seeds.
Uncle Willie let me steer the tractor!

"Uncle Willie planted all kinds of seeds.
I planted one pumpkin seed. It would take
all summer to grow.
I hoped it would grow into a big pumpkin.

"Uncle Willie finished planting.
He asked me to drive to the barn and get the wagon.
He wanted to pick his vegetables and take them to market.

"We filled the wagon with vegetables
from Uncle Willie's garden.
Uncle Willie sat on top of them so that
none would fall off. Then we drove to
the farmers' market.

spinach

cabbage

cauliflower

potatoes

turnip

asparagus

beans

"At the market I parked right next to a water hydrant," said Huckle.
"I delivered the vegetables to Uncle Willie's vegetable stand.

celery

tomatoes

lettuce

corn

beets

squash

peas

UNCLE WILLIE'S VEGETABLES

carrots

onions

FARMERS' MARKET
FRUIT STAND

plums blueberries cherries pears grapes banana

raspberries tangerines apples oranges peaches

pineapple strawberries lemons grapefruit watermelon

"Well! That was the end of my summer vacation," said Huckle.
"I was sent back home. Uncle Willie promised to bring my pumpkin
to me when it was fully grown.

"And he did!
And now I am going to show it to you!
I am also going to show you
what I made with it!"

Why, Huckle! That just has to be the BIGGEST jack-o-lantern ever!
You are not only a good pumpkin grower, you are also
a good jack-o-lantern maker! Isn't he, children?
But be careful that you don't frighten that witch with it!

Learning to Write
Learning to print

When the letters of the alphabet are written,
they look different from letters that are printed.
Written letters are connected to each other.

Miss Honey is going to teach her class how to write.
The first letter in your name is always a big capital letter.
The others are small letters.

This is how Albert's name looks printed: | Albert

And this is how it looks written: | *Albert*

a a
A a

Albert has an apple in his hand
Albert has an apple in his hand

B b
B b

Bananas Gorilla is being silly
Bananas Gorilla is being silly

C c
C c

Charlie Anteater is chewing gum
Charlie Anteater is chewing gum

That is very nice writing, boys!

"Now, Huckle," said Miss Honey, "will you please write all the letters of the alphabet? I want all the children to copy them. With a little help, maybe they will be able to write their own names."

sharpen your pencil!

Aa Bb Cc Dd

Aa Bb Cc Dd

Ee Ff Gg Hh

Ee Ff Gg Hh

Ii Jj Kk Ll

Ii Jj Kk Ll

Mm Nn Oo Pp

Mm Nn Oo Pp

Qq Rr Ss Tt

Qq Rr Ss Tt

Uu Vv Ww Xx

Uu Vv Ww Xx

Yy Zz

Yy Zz

Now, everyone,
please take a pencil and a paper
and try to write your own name.

Visiting the Doctor's Office

From time to time all the children must visit the doctor.
He examines them to make sure that they are well and healthy.
This was the day for Doctor Bear to look at them and make them say AHHHH.
All right! Everyone get in line and file into the doctor's office.
Take off your shirts and blouses.

height measure

scales

Nurse Nelly measured the children to see
how tall they were growing. She weighed
them to see how heavy they were.

Doctor Bear made everyone say AHHHH. He looked
inside their throats. He held his stethoscope
against their bare chests and listened. It tickled.

Doctor Bear said that everyone
was well and healthy.

bandages

scissors

thermometer

flashlight

tongue
stick

adhesive tape

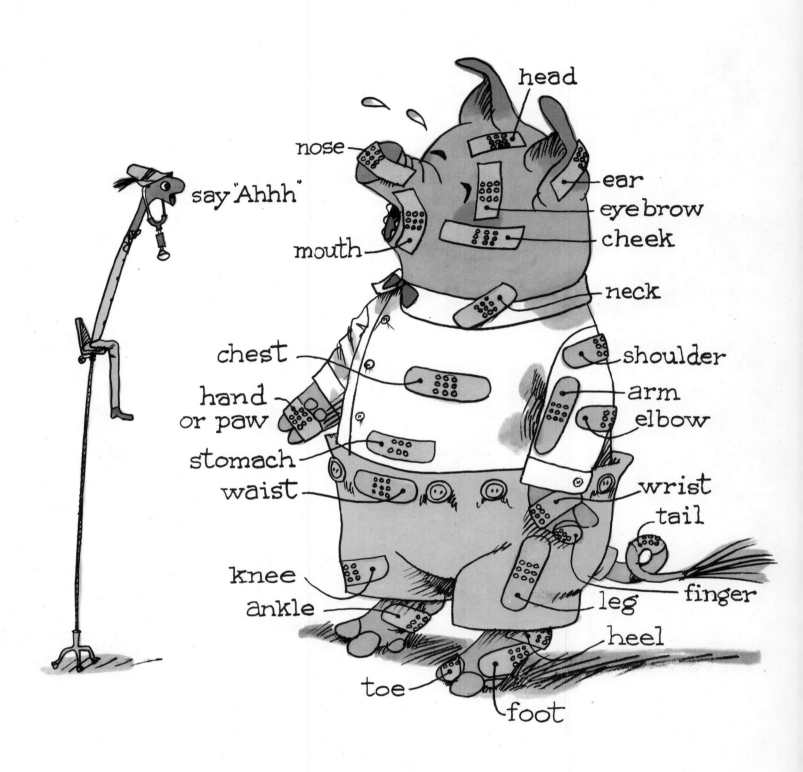

head

nose

say "Ahhh"

ear

eyebrow

cheek

mouth

neck

chest

shoulder

hand
or paw

arm

elbow

stomach

waist

wrist

tail

knee

ankle

leg

finger

heel

toe

foot

The doctor comes to visit the school
only on certain days.
But Nurse Nelly is at school every day.
She looks after any child who isn't feeling well.
Arthur Pig fell down and hurt himself in the schoolyard.
    "Where does it hurt?" Nurse Nelly asked Arthur.
    "Everywhere!" said Arthur.
    So Nurse Nelly put bandages everywhere
to make him stop hurting.

57

Janitor Joe and the Months of the Year

Joe is our school janitor.
A janitor takes care of the schoolhouse.
He fixes things when they get broken.
He works around the school all twelve
months of the year.

The first month of the year is **January.** January is a snowy month.
When it snows, Joe shovels a path through the deep snow.

In **February** he spreads sand on the icy sidewalk so that no one will slip.

What happened?
Did you slip, Joe?

In **March** the strong winds blow.
Joe empties the wastebaskets into the trash burner outside.

In **April** the rain falls from the sky and makes the plants grow.
Joe makes sure that the plants growing in the school flower garden
get plenty of water.

The Easter Bunny
comes in April

In **May** Joe mows the school lawn with his lawnmower.
Once the mower got away and ran into a supermarket.
Do you suppose it was tired of chewing on nothing but grass?

In **June** Miss Honey asked Joe to fix a table.
One leg wobbled a little bit.

Well he really fixed that table, didn't he?
You can fix it correctly during our summer vacation.
We will see you in the fall. Keep the school looking nice, Joe!

In **July,** when everyone
was away on vacation,
Joe gave everything
a fresh coat of paint.

The month of **August** is very hot and sunny.
That's when Joe fixed the showers in the gym.
He pretended that he was at the seashore.

In **September** school begins again.
Joe made a new cement sidewalk for the children to walk on.
It is now soft and wet. Tomorrow it will be hard and dry.
I think you should have made it a few days sooner, Joe!

nice work, Joe!

In **October,** the leaves begin to fall. Joe raked them up
and carried them in his wheelbarrow to a big pile.
He burned them in an open place so nothing else would catch fire.

I love the smell of burning leaves.

JOE! You left the wheelbarrow
too close to the fire!

November is a cold and windy month. Winter is coming.
Joe sawed the dead branches off the trees so they
wouldn't be broken off by the wind and fall on top of something.
The principal came out to look at his new car.

In **December** there are
lots of holiday celebrations.
Joe put up the
school Christmas tree.
He decorated it
with ornaments.
It looks beautiful.
So far Joe has done
something right
for a change.
He has only
to put the star
on the top of the tree.
Can you reach it, Joe?